Marjorie's Three Gifts

Louisa May Alcott

Contents

MARJORIE'S THREE GIFTS 7

ROSES AND FORGET-ME-NOTS 18

I. ROSES 18

II. FORGET-ME-NOTS 25

MARJORIE'S THREE GIFTS

BY

Louisa May Alcott

MARJORIE'S THREE GIFTS

Marjorie sat on the door-step, shelling peas, quite unconscious what a pretty picture she made, with the roses peeping at her through the lattice work of the porch, the wind playing hide-and-seek in her curly hair, while the sunshine with its silent magic changed her faded gingham to a golden gown, and shimmered on the bright tin pan as if it were a silver shield. Old Rover lay at her feet, the white kitten purred on her shoulder, and friendly robins hopped about her in the grass, chirping "A happy birthday, Marjorie!"

But the little maid neither saw nor heard, for her eyes were fixed on the green pods, and her thoughts were far away. She was recalling the fairy-tale granny told her last night, and wishing with all her heart that such things happened nowadays. For in this story, as a poor girl like herself sat spinning before the door, a Brownie came by, and gave the child a good-luck penny; then a fairy passed, and left a talisman which would keep her always happy; and last of all, the prince rolled up in his chariot, and took her away to reign with him over a lovely kingdom, as a reward for her many kindnesses to others.

When Marjorie imagined this part of the story, it was impossible to help giving one little sigh, and for a minute she forgot her work, so busy was she thinking what beautiful presents she would give to all the poor children in her realm when THEY had birthdays. Five impatient young peas took this opportunity to escape from the half-open pod in her hand and skip down the steps, to be immediately gobbled up by an audacious robin, who gave thanks in such a shrill chirp that Marjorie woke up, laughed, and fell to work again. She was just finishing, when a voice called out from the lane,--

"Hi, there! come here a minute, child!" and looking up, she saw a little old man in a queer little carriage drawn by a fat little pony.

Running down to the gate, Marjorie dropped a curtsy, saying pleasantly,--

"What did you wish, sir?"

"Just undo that check-rein for me. I am lame, and Jack wants to drink at your brook," answered the old man, nodding at her till his spectacles danced on his nose.

Marjorie was rather afraid of the fat pony, who tossed his head, whisked his tail, and stamped his feet as if he was of a peppery temper. But she liked to be useful, and just then felt as if there were few things she could NOT do if she tried, because it was her birthday. So she proudly let down the rein, and when Jack went splashing into the brook, she stood on the bridge, waiting to check him up again after he had drunk his fill of the clear, cool water.

The old gentleman sat in his place, looking up at the little girl, who was smiling to herself as she watched the blue dragon-flies dance among the ferns, a blackbird tilt on the alderboughs, and listened to the babble of the brook.

"How old are you, child?" asked the old man, as if he rather envied this rosy creature her youth and health.

"Twelve to-day, sir;" and Marjorie stood up straight and tall, as if mindful of her years.

"Had any presents?" asked the old man, peering up with an odd smile.

"One, sir,--here it is;" and she pulled out of her pocket a tin savings-bank in the shape of a desirable family mansion, painted red, with a green door and black chimney. Proudly displaying it on the rude railing of the bridge, she added, with a happy face,--

"Granny gave it to me, and all the money in it is going to be mine."

"How much have you got?" asked the old gentleman, who appeared to like to sit there in the middle of the brook, while Jack bathed his feet and leisurely gurgled and sneezed.

"Not a penny yet, but I'm going to earn some," answered Marjorie, patting the little bank with an air of resolution pretty to see.

"How will you do it?" continued the inquisitive old man.

"Oh, I'm going to pick berries and dig dandelions, and weed, and drive cows, and do chores. It is vacation, and I can work all the time, and earn ever so much."

"But vacation is play-time,--how about that?"

"Why, that sort of work IS play, and I get bits of fun all along. I always have a good swing when I go for the cows, and pick flowers with the dandelions. Weeding isn't so nice, but berrying is very pleasant, and we have good times all together."

"What shall you do with your money when you get it?"

"Oh, lots of things! Buy books and clothes for school, and, if I get a great deal, give some to granny. I'd love to do that, for she takes care of me, and I'd be so proud to help her!"

"Good little lass!" said the old gentleman, as he put his hand in his pocket. "Would you now?" he added, apparently addressing himself to a large frog who sat upon a stone, looking so wise and grandfatherly that it really did seem quite proper to consult him. At all events, he gave his opinion in the most decided manner, for, with a loud croak, he turned an undignified somersault into the brook, splashing up the water at a great rate. "Well, perhaps it wouldn't be best on the whole. Industry is a good teacher, and money cannot buy happiness, as I know to my sorrow."

The old gentleman still seemed to be talking to the frog, and as he spoke he took his hand out of his pocket with less in it than he had at first intended.

"What a very queer person!" thought Marjorie, for she had not heard a word, and wondered what he was thinking about down there.

Jack walked out of the brook just then, and she ran to check him up; not an easy task for little hands, as he preferred to nibble the grass on the bank. But she did it cleverly, smoothed the ruffled mane, and, dropping another curtsy, stood aside to let the little carriage pass.

"Thank you, child--thank you. Here is something for your bank, and good luck to it."

As he spoke, the old man laid a bright gold dollar in her hand, patted the rosy cheek, and vanished in a cloud of dust, leaving Marjorie so astonished at the grandeur of the gift, that she stood looking at it as if it had been a fortune. It was to her; and visions of pink calico gowns, new grammars, and fresh hat-ribbons danced through her head in delightful confusion, as her eyes rested on the shining coin in her palm.

Then, with a solemn air, she invested her first money by popping it down the chimney of the scarlet mansion, and peeping in with one eye to see if it landed safely on the ground-floor. This done, she took a long breath, and looked over the railing, to be sure it was not all a dream. No; the wheel marks were still there, the brown water was not yet clear, and, if a witness was needed, there sat the big frog again, looking so like the old gentleman, with his bottle-green coat, speckled trousers, and twinkling eyes, that Marjorie burst out laughing, and clapped her hands, saying aloud,--

"I'll play he was the Brownie, and this is the good-luck penny he gave me. Oh, what fun!" and away she skipped, rattling the dear new bank like a castanet.

When she had told granny all about it, she got knife and basket, and went out to dig dandelions; for the desire to increase her fortune was so strong, she could not rest a minute. Up and down she went, so busily peering and digging, that she never lifted up her eyes till something like a great white bird skimmed by so low she could not help seeing it. A pleasant laugh sounded behind her as she started up, and, looking round, she nearly sat down again in sheer surprise, for there close by was a slender little lady, comfortably established under a big umbrella.

"If there WERE any fairies, I'd be sure that was one," thought Marjorie, staring with all her might, for her mind was still full of the old story; and curious things do happen on birthdays, as every one knows.

It really did seem rather elfish to look up suddenly and see a lovely lady all in white, with shining hair and a wand in her hand, sitting under what looked very like a large yellow mushroom in the middle of a meadow, where, till now, nothing but cows and grasshoppers had been seen. Before Marjorie could decide the question, the pleasant laugh came again, and the stranger said, pointing to the white thing that was still fluttering over the grass like a little cloud,--

"Would you kindly catch my hat for me, before it blows quite away?"

Down went basket and knife, and away ran Marjorie, entirely satisfied now that there was no magic about the new-comer; for if she had been an elf, couldn't she have got her hat without any help from a mortal child? Presently, however, it did begin to seem as if that hat was bewitched, for it led the nimble-footed Marjorie such a chase that the cows stopped feeding to look on in placid wonder; the grasshoppers vainly tried to keep up, and every ox-eye daisy did its best to catch the runaway, but failed entirely, for the wind liked a game of romps, and had it that day. As she ran, Marjorie heard the lady singing, like the princess in the story of the Goose-Girl,--

"Blow, breezes, blow!
Let Curdkin's hat go!
Blow, breezes, blow!
Let him after it go!
O'er hills, dales and rocks,
Away be it whirled,
Till the silvery locks
Are all combed and curled."

This made her laugh so that she tumbled into a clover-bed, and lay there a minute to get her breath. Just then, as if the playful wind repented of its frolic, the long veil fastened to the hat caught in a blackberry-vine near by, and held the truant fast till Marjorie secured it.

"Now come and see what I am doing," said the lady, when she had thanked the child.

Marjorie drew near confidingly, and looked down at the wide-spread book before her. She gave a start, and laughed out with surprise and delight; for there was a lovely picture of her own little home, and her own little self on the door-step, all so delicate, and beautiful, and true, it seemed as if done by magic.

"Oh, how pretty! There is Rover, and Kitty and the robins, and me! How could you ever do it, ma'am?" said Marjorie, with a wondering glance at the long paint-brush, which had wrought what seemed a miracle to her childish eyes.

"I'll show you presently; but tell me, first, if it looks quite right and natural to you. Children sometimes spy out faults that no one else can see," answered the lady, evidently pleased with the artless praise her work received.

"It looks just like our house, only more beautiful. Perhaps that is because I know how shabby it really is. That moss looks lovely on the shingles, but the roof leaks. The porch is broken, only the roses hide the place; and my gown is all faded, though it once was as bright as you have made it. I wish the house and everything would stay pretty forever, as they will in the picture."

While Marjorie spoke, the lady had been adding more color to the sketch, and when she looked up, something warmer and brighter than sunshine shone in her face, as she said, so cheerily, it was like a bird's song to hear her,--

"It can't be summer always, dear, but we can make fair weather for ourselves if we try. The moss, the roses, and soft shadows show the little house and the little girl at their best, and that is what we all should do; for it is amazing how lovely common things become, if one only knows how to look at them."

"I wish _I_ did," said Marjorie, half to herself, remembering how often she was discontented, and how hard it was to get on, sometimes.

"So do I," said the lady, in her happy voice. "Just believe that there is a sunny side to everything, and try to find it, and you will be surprised to see how bright the world will seem, and how cheerful you will be able to keep your little self."

"I guess granny has found that out, for she never frets. I do, but I'm going to stop it, because I'm twelve to-day, and that is too old for such

things," said Marjorie, recollecting the good resolutions she had made
that morning when she woke.

"I am twice twelve, and not entirely cured yet; but I try, and don't
mean to wear blue spectacles if I can help it," answered the lady, laughing so blithely that Marjorie was sure she would not have to try much
longer. "Birthdays were made for presents, and I should like to give you
one. Would it please you to have this little picture?" she added, lifting
it out of the book.

"Truly my own? Oh, yes, indeed!" cried Marjorie, coloring with
pleasure, for she had never owned so beautiful a thing before.

"Then you shall have it, dear. Hang it where you can see it often,
and when you look, remember that it is the sunny side of home, and
help to keep it so."

Marjorie had nothing but a kiss to offer by way of thanks, as the
lovely sketch was put into her hand; but the giver seemed quite satisfied,
for it was a very grateful little kiss. Then the child took up her basket
and went away, not dancing and singing now, but slowly and silently;
for this gift made her thoughtful as well as glad. As she climbed the wall,
she looked back to nod good-by to the pretty lady; but the meadow was
empty, and all she saw was the grass blowing in the wind.

"Now, deary, run out and play, for birthdays come but once a year,
and we must make them as merry as we can," said granny, as she settled
herself for her afternoon nap, when the Saturday cleaning was all done,
and the little house as neat as wax.

So Marjorie put on a white apron in honor of the occasion, and, taking Kitty in her arms, went out to enjoy herself. Three swings on the
gate seemed to be a good way of beginning the festivities; but she only
got two, for when the gate creaked back the second time, it stayed shut,
and Marjorie hung over the pickets, arrested by the sound of music.

"It's soldiers," she said, as the fife and drum drew nearer, and flags were seen waving over the barberry-bushes at the corner.

"No; it's a picnic," she added in a moment; for she saw hats with wreaths about them bobbing up and down, as a gayly-trimmed hay-cart full of children came rumbling down the lane.

"What a nice time they are going to have!" thought Marjorie, sadly contrasting that merry-making with the quiet party she was having all by herself.

Suddenly her face shone, and Kitty was waved over her head like a banner, as she flew out of the gate, crying, rapturously,--

"It's Billy! and I know he's come for me!"

It certainly WAS Billy, proudly driving the old horse, and beaming at his little friend from the bower of flags and chestnut-boughs, where he sat in state, with a crown of daisies on his sailor-hat and a spray of blooming sweetbrier in his hand. Waving his rustic sceptre, he led off the shout of "Happy birthday, Marjorie!" which was set up as the wagon stopped at the gate, and the green boughs suddenly blossomed with familiar faces, all smiling on the little damsel, who stood in the lane quite overpowered with delight.

"It's a s'prise party!" cried one small lad, tumbling out behind.

"We are going up the mountain to have fun!" added a chorus of voices, as a dozen hands beckoned wildly.

"We got it up on purpose for you, so tie your hat and come away," said a pretty girl, leaning down to kiss Marjorie, who had dropped Kitty, and stood ready for any splendid enterprise.

A word to granny, and away went the happy child, sitting up beside Billy, under the flags that waved over a happier load than any royal chariot ever bore.

It would be vain to try and tell all the plays and pleasures of happy children on a Saturday afternoon, but we may briefly say that Marjorie found a mossy stone all ready for her throne, and Billy crowned her with a garland like his own. That a fine banquet was spread, and eaten with a relish many a Lord Mayor's feast has lacked. Then how the whole court danced and played together afterward! The lords climbed trees and turned somersaults, the ladies gathered flowers and told secrets under the sweetfern-bushes, the queen lost her shoe jumping over the waterfall, and the king paddled into the pool below and rescued it. A happy little kingdom, full of summer sunshine, innocent delights, and loyal hearts; for love ruled, and the only war that disturbed the peaceful land was waged by the mosquitoes as night came on.

Marjorie stood on her throne watching the sunset while her maids of honor packed up the remains of the banquet, and her knights prepared the chariot. All the sky was gold and purple, all the world bathed in a soft, red light, and the little girl was very happy as she looked down at the subjects who had served her so faithfully that day.

"Have you had a good time, Marjy?" asked King William; who stood below, with his royal nose on a level with her majesty's two dusty little shoes.

"Oh, Billy, it has been just splendid! But I don't see why you should all be so kind to me," answered Marjorie, with such a look of innocent wonder, that Billy laughed to see it.

"Because you are so sweet and good, we can't help loving you,--that's why," he said, as if this simple fact was reason enough.

"I'm going to be the best girl that ever was, and love everybody in the world," cried the child, stretching out her arms as if ready, in the fulness of her happy heart, to embrace all creation.

"Don't turn into an angel and fly away just yet, but come home, or granny will never lend you to us any more."

With that, Billy jumped her down, and away they ran, to ride gayly back through the twilight, singing like a flock of nightingales.

As she went to bed that night, Marjorie looked at the red bank, the pretty picture, and the daisy crown, saying to herself,--

"It has been a VERY nice birthday, and I am something like the girl in the story, after all, for the old man gave me a good-luck penny, the kind lady told me how to keep happy, and Billy came for me like the prince. The girl didn't go back to the poor house again, but I'm glad _I_ did, for MY granny isn't a cross one, and my little home is the dearest in the world."

Then she tied her night-cap, said her prayers, and fell asleep; but the moon, looking in to kiss the blooming face upon the pillow, knew that three good spirits had come to help little Marjorie from that day forth, and their names were Industry, Cheerfulness, and Love.

ROSES AND FORGET-ME-NOTS

I. ROSES

It was a cold November storm, and everything looked forlorn. Even the pert sparrows were draggle-tailed and too much out of spirits to fight for crumbs with the fat pigeons who tripped through the mud with their little red boots as if in haste to get back to their cosy home in the dove-cot.

But the most forlorn creature out that day was a small errand girl, with a bonnet-box on each arm, and both hands struggling to hold a big broken umbrella. A pair of worn-out boots let in the wet upon her tired feet; a thin cotton dress and an old shawl poorly protected her from the storm; and a faded hood covered her head.

The face that looked out from this hood was too pale and anxious for one so young; and when a sudden gust turned the old umbrella inside out with a crash, despair fell upon poor Lizzie, and she was so miserable she could have sat down in the rain and cried.

But there was no time for tears; so, dragging the dilapidated umbrella along, she spread her shawl over the bonnet-boxes and hurried down the broad street, eager to hide her misfortunes from a pretty young girl who stood at a window laughing at her.

She could not find the number of the house where one of the fine hats was to be left; and after hunting all down one side of the street, she crossed over, and came at last to the very house where the pretty girl lived. She was no longer to be seen; and, with a sigh of relief, Lizzie rang the bell, and was told to wait in the hall while Miss Belle tried the hat on.

Glad to rest, she warmed her feet, righted her umbrella, and then sat looking about her with eyes quick to see the beauty and the comfort that made the place so homelike and delightful. A small waiting-room opened from the hall, and in it stood many blooming plants, whose fragrance attracted Lizzie as irresistibly as if she had been a butterfly or bee.

Slipping in, she stood enjoying the lovely colors, sweet odors, and delicate shapes of these household spirits; for Lizzie loved flowers passionately; and just then they possessed a peculiar charm for her.

One particularly captivating little rose won her heart, and made her long for it with a longing that became a temptation too strong to resist. It was so perfect; so like a rosy face smiling out from the green leaves, that Lizzie could NOT keep her hands off it, and having smelt, touched, and kissed it, she suddenly broke the stem and hid it in her pocket. Then, frightened at what she had done, she crept back to her place in the hall, and sat there, burdened with remorse.

A servant came just then to lead her upstairs; for Miss Belle wished the hat altered, and must give directions. With her heart in a flutter, and pinker roses in her cheeks than the one in her pocket, Lizzie followed to a handsome room, where a pretty girl stood before a long mirror with the hat in her hand.

"Tell Madame Tifany that I don't like it at all, for she hasn't put in the blue plume mamma ordered; and I won't have rose-buds, they are so common," said the young lady, in a dissatisfied tone, as she twirled the hat about.

"Yes, miss," was all Lizzie could say; for SHE considered that hat the loveliest thing a girl could possibly own.

"You had better ask your mamma about it, Miss Belle, before you give any orders. She will be up in a few moments, and the girl can wait," put in a maid, who was sewing in the ante-room.

"I suppose I must; but I WON'T have roses," answered Belle, crossly. Then she glanced at Lizzie, and said more gently, "You look very cold; come and sit by the fire while you wait."

"I'm afraid I'll wet the pretty rug, miss; my feet are sopping," said Lizzie, gratefully, but timidly.

"So they are! Why didn't you wear rubber boots?"

"I haven't got any."

"I'll give you mine, then, for I hate them; and as I never go out in wet weather, they are of no earthly use to me. Marie, bring them here; I shall be glad to get rid of them, and I'm sure they'll be useful to you."

"Oh, thank you, miss! I'd like 'em ever so much, for I'm out in the rain half the time, and get bad colds because my boots are old," said Lizzie, smiling brightly at the thought of the welcome gift.

"I should think your mother would get you warmer things," began Belle, who found something rather interesting in the shabby girl, with shy bright eyes, and curly hair bursting out of the old hood.

"I haven't got any mother," said Lizzie, with a pathetic glance at her poor clothes.

"I'm so sorry! Have you brothers and sisters?" asked Belle, hoping to find something pleasant to talk about; for she was a kind little soul.

"No, miss; I've got no folks at all."

"Oh, dear; how sad! Why, who takes care of you?" cried Belle, looking quite distressed.

"No one; I take care of myself. I work for Madame, and she pays me a dollar a week. I stay with Mrs. Brown, and chore round to pay for my keep. My dollar don't get many clothes, so I can't be as neat as I'd like." And the forlorn look came back to poor Lizzie's face.

Belle said nothing, but sat among the sofa cushions, where she had thrown herself, looking soberly at this other girl, no older than she was, who took care of herself and was all alone in the world. It was a new idea to Belle, who was loved and petted as an only child is apt to be. She often saw beggars and pitied them, but knew very little about their wants and lives; so it was like turning a new page in her happy life to be brought so near to poverty as this chance meeting with the milliner's girl.

"Aren't you afraid and lonely and unhappy?" she said, slowly, trying to understand and put herself in Lizzie's place.

"Yes; but it's no use. I can't help it, and may be things will get better by and by, and I'll have my wish," answered Lizzie, more hopefully, because Belle's pity warmed her heart and made her troubles seem lighter.

"What is your wish?" asked Belle, hoping mamma wouldn't come just yet, for she was getting interested in the stranger.

"To have a nice little room, and make flowers, like a French girl I know. It's such pretty work, and she gets lots of money, for every one likes her flowers. She shows me how, sometimes, and I can do leaves first-rate; but--"

There Lizzie stopped suddenly, and the color rushed up to her forehead; for she remembered the little rose in her pocket and it weighed upon her conscience like a stone.

Before Belle could ask what was the matter, Marie came in with a tray of cake and fruit, saying:

"Here's your lunch, Miss Belle."

"Put it down, please; I'm not ready for it yet."

And Belle shook her head as she glanced at Lizzie, who was staring hard at the fire with such a troubled face that Belle could not bear to see it.

Jumping out of her nest of cushions, she heaped a plate with good things, and going to Lizzie, offered it, saying, with a gentle courtesy that made the act doubly sweet:

"Please have some; you must be tired of waiting."

But Lizzie could not take it; she could only cover her face and cry; for this kindness rent her heart and made the stolen flower a burden too heavy to be borne.

"Oh, don't cry so! Are you sick? Have I been rude? Tell me all about it; and if I can't do anything, mamma can," said Belle, surprised and troubled.

"No; I'm not sick; I'm bad, and I can't bear it when you are so good to me," sobbed Lizzie, quite overcome with penitence; and taking out the crumpled rose, she confessed her fault with many tears.

"Don't feel so much about such a little thing as that," began Belle, warmly; then checked herself, and added, more soberly, "It WAS wrong to take it without leave; but it's all right now, and I'll give you as many roses as you want, for I know you are a good girl."

"Thank you. I didn't want it only because it was pretty, but I wanted to copy it. I can't get any for myself, and so I can't do my make-believe ones well. Madame won't even lend me the old ones in the store, and Estelle has none to spare for me, because I can't pay her for teaching me. She gives me bits of muslin and wire and things, and shows me now and then. But I know if I had a real flower I could copy it; so she'd see I did know something, for I try real hard. I'm SO tired of slopping round the streets, I'd do anything to earn my living some other way."

Lizzie had poured out her trouble rapidly; and the little story was quite affecting when one saw the tears on her cheeks, the poor clothes, and the thin hands that held the stolen rose. Belle was much touched, and, in her impetuous way, set about mending matters as fast as possible.

"Put on those boots and that pair of dry stockings right away. Then tuck as much cake and fruit into your pocket as it will hold. I'm going to get you some flowers, and see if mamma is too busy to attend to me."

With a nod and a smile, Belle flew about the room a minute; then vanished, leaving Lizzie to her comfortable task, feeling as if fairies still haunted the world as in the good old times.

When Belle came back with a handful of roses, she found Lizzie absorbed in admiring contemplation of her new boots, as she ate sponge-cake in a blissful sort of waking-dream.

"Mamma can't come; but I don't care about the hat. It will do very well, and isn't worth fussing about. There, will those be of any use to you?" And she offered the nosegay with a much happier face than the one Lizzie first saw.

"Oh, miss, they're just lovely! I'll copy that pink rose as soon as ever I can, and when I've learned how to do 'em tip-top, I'd like to bring you some, if you don't mind," answered Lizzie, smiling all over her face as she buried her nose luxuriously in the fragrant mass.

"I'd like it very much, for I should think you'd have to be very clever to make such pretty things. I really quite fancy those rosebuds in my hat, now I know that you're going to learn how to make them. Put an orange in your pocket, and the flowers in water as soon as you can, so they'll be fresh when you want them. Good-by. Bring home our hats every time and tell me how you get on."

With kind words like these, Belle dismissed Lizzie, who ran downstairs, feeling as rich as if she had found a fortune. Away to the next place she hurried, anxious to get her errands done and the precious posy safely into fresh water. But Mrs. Turretviile was not at home, and the bonnet could not be left till paid for. So Lizzie turned to go down the high steps, glad that she need not wait. She stopped one instant to take a delicious sniff at her flowers, and that was the last happy moment that poor Lizzie knew for many weary months.

The new boots were large for her, the steps slippery with sleet, and down went the little errand girl, from top to bottom, till she landed in the gutter directly upon Mrs. Turretville's costly bonnet.

"I've saved my posies, anyway," sighed Lizzie, as she picked herself up, bruised, wet, and faint with pain; "but, oh, my heart! won't Madame scold when she sees that band-box smashed flat," groaned the poor child, sitting on the curbstone to get her breath and view the disaster.

The rain poured, the wind blew, the sparrows on the park railing chirped derisively, and no one came along to help Lizzie out of her troubles. Slowly she gathered up her burdens; painfully she limped away in the big boots; and the last the naughty sparrows saw of her was a shabby little figure going round the corner, with a pale, tearful face held lovingly over the bright bouquet that was her one treasure and her only comfort in the moment which brought to her the great misfortune of her life.

II. FORGET-ME-NOTS

"Oh, mamma, I am so relieved that the box has come at last! If it had not, I do believe I should have died of disappointment," cried pretty Belle, five years later, on the morning before her eighteenth birthday.

"It would have been a serious disappointment, darling; for I had sot my heart on your wearing my gift to-morrow night, and when the steamers kept coming in without my trunk from Paris, I was very anxious. I hope you will like it."

"Dear mamma, I know I shall like it; your taste is so good and you know what suits me so well. Make haste, Marie; I'm dying to see it," said Belle, dancing about the great trunk, as the maid carefully unfolded tissue papers and muslin wrappers.

A young girl's first ball-dress is a grand affair,--in her eyes, at least; and Belle soon stopped dancing, to stand with clasped hands, eager eyes and parted lips before the snowy pile of illusion that was at last daintily lifted out upon the bed. Then, as Marie displayed its loveliness, little cries of delight were heard, and when the whole delicate dress was arranged to the best effect she threw herself upon her mother's neck and actually cried with pleasure.

"Mamma, it is too lovely I and you are very kind to do so much for me. How shall I ever thank you?"

"By putting it right on to see if it fits; and when you wear it look your happiest, that I may be proud of my pretty daughter."

Mamma got no further, for Marie uttered a French shriek, wrung her hands, and then began to burrow wildly in the trunk and among the papers, crying distractedly:

"Great Heavens, madame! the wreath has been forgotten! What an affliction! Mademoiselle's enchanting toilette is destroyed without the wreath, and nowhere do I find it."

In vain they searched; in vain Marie wailed and Belle declared it must be somewhere; no wreath appeared. It was duly set down in the bill, and a fine sum charged for a head-dress to match the dainty forget-me-nots that looped the fleecy skirts and ornamented the bosom of the dress. It had evidently been forgotten; and mamma despatched Marie at once to try and match the flowers, for Belle would not hear of any other decoration for her beautiful blonde hair.

The dress fitted to a charm, and was pronounced by all beholders the loveliest thing ever seen. Nothing was wanted but the wreath to make it quite perfect, and when Marie returned, after a long search, with no forget-me-nots, Belle was in despair.

"Wear natural ones," suggested a sympathizing friend.

But another hunt among greenhouses was as fruitless as that among the milliners' rooms. No forget-me-nots could be found, and Marie fell exhausted into a chair, desolated at what she felt to be an awful calamity.

"Let me have the carriage, and I'll ransack the city till I find some," cried Belle, growing more resolute with each failure.

Marnma was deep in preparations for the ball, and could not help her afflicted daughter, though she was much disappointed at the mishap. So Belle drove off, resolved to have her flowers whether there were any or not.

Any one who has ever tried to match a ribbon, find a certain fabric, or get anything done in a hurry, knows what a wearisome task it sometimes is, and can imagine Belle's state of mind after repeated disappointments. She was about to give up in despair, when some one suggested that perhaps the Frenchwoman, Estelle Valnor, might make the desired wreath, if there was time.

Away drove Belle, and, on entering the room, gave a sigh of satisfaction, for a whole boxful of the loveliest forget-me-nots stood upon the table. As fast as possible, she told her tale and demanded the flowers, no matter what the price might be. Imagine her feelings when the Frenchwoman, with a shrug, announced that it was impossible to give mademoiselle a single spray. All were engaged to trim a bridesmaid's dress, and must be sent away at once.

It really was too bad! and Belle lost her temper entirely, for no persuasion or bribes would win a spray from Estelle. The provoking part of it was that the wedding would not come off for several days, and there was time enough to make more flowers for that dress, since Belle only wanted a few for her hair. Neither would Estelle make her any, as her hands were full, and so small an order was not worth deranging one's self for; but observing Belle's sorrowful face, she said, affably:

"Mademoiselle may, perhaps, find the flowers she desires at Miss Berton's. She has been helping me with these garlands, and may have some left. Here is her address."

Belle took the card with thanks, and hurried away with a last hope faintly stirring in her girlish heart, for Belle had an unusually ardent wish to look her best at this party, since Somebody was to be there, and Somebody considered forget-me-nots the sweetest flowers in the world. Mamma knew this, and the kiss Belle gave her when the dress came had a more tender meaning than gratified vanity or daughterly love.

Up many stairs she climbed, and came at last to a little room, very poor but very neat, where, at the one window, sat a young girl, with crutches by her side and her lap full of flower-leaves and petals. She rose slowly as Belle came in, and then stood looking at her, with such a wistful expression in her shy, bright eyes, that Belle's anxious face cleared involuntarily, and her voice lost its impatient tone.

As she spoke, she glanced about the room, hoping to see some blue blossoms awaiting her. But none appeared; and she was about to despond again, when the girl said, gently:

"I have none by me now, but I may be able to find you some."

"Thank you very much; but I have been everywhere in vain. Still, if you do get any, please send them to me as soon as possible. Here is my card."

Miss Berton glanced at it, then cast a quick look at the sweet, anxious face before her, and smiled so brightly that Belle smiled also, and asked, wonderingly:

"What is it? What do you see?"

"I see the dear young lady who was so kind to me long ago. You don't remember me, and never knew my name; but I never have forgotten you all these years. I always hoped I could do something to show how grateful I was, and now I can, for you shall have your flowers if I sit up all night to make them."

But Belle still shook her head and watched the smiling face before her with wondering eyes, till the girl added, with sudden color in her cheeks:

"Ah, you've done so many kind things in your life, you don't remember the little errand girl from Madame Tifany's who stole a rose in your hall, and how you gave her rubber boots and cake and flowers, and were so good to her she couldn't forget it if she lived to be a hundred."

"But you are so changed," began Belle, who did faintly recollect that little incident in her happy life.

"Yes, I had a fall and hurt myself so that I shall always be lame."

And Lizzie went on to tell how Madame had dismissed her in a rage; how she lay ill till Mrs. Brown sent her to the hospital; and how for a year she had suffered much alone, in that great house of pain, before one of the kind visitors had befriended her.

While hearing the story of the five years, that had been so full of pleasure, ease and love for herself, Belle forgot her errand, and, sitting beside Lizzie, listened with pitying eyes to all she told of her endeavors to support herself by the delicate handiwork she loved.

"I'm very happy now," ended Lizzie, looking about the little bare room with a face full of the sweetest content. "I get nearly work enough to pay my way, and Estelle sends me some when she has more than she can do. I've learned to do it nicely, and it is so pleasant to sit here and make flowers instead of trudging about in the wet with other people's hats. Though I do sometimes wish I was able to trudge, one gets on so slowly with crutches."

A little sigh followed the words, and Belle put her own plump hand on the delicate one that held the crutch, saying, in her cordial young voice:

"I'll come and take you to drive sometimes, for you are too pale, and you'll get ill sitting here at work day after day. Please let me; I'd love to; for I feel so idle and wicked when I see busy people like you that I reproach myself for neglecting my duty and having more than my share of happiness."

Lizzie thanked her with a look, and then said, in a tone of interest that was delightful to hear:

"Tell about the wreath you want; I should so love to do it for you, if I can."

Belle had forgotten all about it in listening to this sad little story of a girl's life. Now she felt half ashamed to talk of so frivolous a matter till she remembered that it would help Lizzie; and, resolving to pay for it as never garland was paid for before, she entered upon the subject with renewed interest.

"You shall have the flowers in time for your ball to-morrow night. I will engage to make a wreath that will please you, only it may take longer than I think. Don't be troubled if I don't send it till evening; it will surely come in time. I can work fast, and this will be the happiest job I ever did," said Lizzie, beginning to lay out mysterious little tools and bend delicate wires.

"You are altogether too grateful for the little I have done. It makes me feel ashamed to think I did not find you out before and do something better worth thanks."

"Ah, it wasn't the boots or the cake or the roses, dear Miss Belle. It was the kind looks, the gentle words, the way it was done, that went right to my heart, and did me more good than a million of money. I never stole a pin after that day, for the little rose wouldn't let me forget how you forgave me so sweetly. I sometimes think it kept me from greater temptations, for I was a poor, forlorn child, with no one to keep me good."

Pretty Belle looked prettier than ever as she listened, and a bright tear stood in either eye like a drop of dew on a blue flower. It touched her very much to learn that her little act of childish charity had been so sweet and helpful to this lonely girl, and now lived so freshly in her grateful memory. It showed her, suddenly, how precious little deeds of love and sympathy are; how strong to bless, how easy to perform, how comfortable to recall. Her heart was very full and tender just then, and the lesson sunk deep into it never to be forgotten.

She sat a long time watching flowers bud and blossom under Lizzie's skilful fingers, and then hurried home to tell all her glad news to mamma.

If the next day had not been full of most delightfully exciting events, Belle might have felt some anxiety about her wreath, for hour after hour went by and nothing arrived from Lizzie.

Evening came, and all was ready. Belle was dressed, and looked so lovely that mamma declared she needed nothing more. But Marie insisted that the grand effect would be ruined without the garland among the sunshiny hair. Belle had time now to be anxious, and waited with growing impatience for the finishing touch to her charming toilette.

"I must be downstairs to receive, and can't wait another moment; so put in the blue pompon and let me go," she said at last, with a sigh of disappointment, for the desire to look beautiful that night in Somebody's eyes had increased four-fold.

With a tragic gesture, Marie was about to adjust the pompon when the quick tap of a crutch came down the hall, and Lizzie hurried in, flushed and breathless, but smiling happily as she uncovered the box she carried with a look of proud satisfaction.

A general "Ah!" of admiration arose as Belle, mamma, and Marie surveyed the lovely wreath that lay before them; and when it was carefully arranged on the bright head that was to wear it, Belle blushed with pleasure. Mamma said: "It is more beautiful than any Paris could have sent us;" and Marie clasped her hands theatrically, sighing, with her head on one side:

"Truly, yes; mademoiselle is now adorable!"

"I am so glad you like it. I did my very best and worked all night, but I had to beg one spray from Estelle, or, with all my haste, I could not have finished in time," said Lizzie, refreshing her weary eyes with a long, affectionate gaze at the pretty figure before her.

A fold of the airy skirt was caught on one of the blue clusters, and

Lizzie knelt down to arrange it as she spoke. Belle leaned toward her and said softly: "Money alone can't pay you for this kindness; so tell me how I can best serve you. This is the happiest night of my life, and I want to make every one feel glad also."

"Then don't talk of paying me, but promise that I may make the flowers you wear on your wedding-day," whispered Lizzie, kissing the kind hand held out to help her rise, for on it she saw a brilliant ring, and in the blooming, blushing face bent over her she read the tender little story that Somebody had told Belle that day.

"So you shall! and I'll keep this wreath all my life for your sake, dear," answered Belle, as her full heart bubbled over with pitying affection for the poor girl who would never make a bridal garland for herself.

Belle kept her word, even when she was in a happy home of her own; for out of the dead roses bloomed a friendship that brightened Lizzie's life; and long after the blue garland was faded Belle remembered the helpful little lesson that taught her to read the faces poverty touches with a pathetic eloquence, which says to those who look, "Forget-me-not."

The Codes Of Hammurabi And Moses
W. W. Davies

QTY

The discovery of the Hammurabi Code is one of the greatest achievements of archaeology, and is of paramount interest, not only to the student of the Bible, but also to all those interested in ancient history...

Religion   **ISBN:** *1-59462-338-4*   **Pages:132**

MSRP $12.95

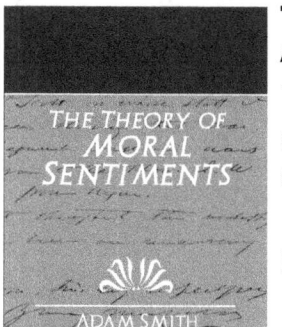

The Theory of Moral Sentiments
Adam Smith

QTY

This work from 1749. contains original theories of conscience amd moral judgment and it is the foundation for systemof morals.

Philosophy   **ISBN:** *1-59462-777-0*   **Pages:536**

MSRP $19.95

Jessica's First Prayer
Hesba Stretton

QTY

In a screened and secluded corner of one of the many railway-bridges which span the streets of London there could be seen a few years ago, from five o'clock every morning until half past eight, a tidily set-out coffee-stall, consisting of a trestle and board, upon which stood two large tin cans, with a small fire of charcoal burning under each so as to keep the coffee boiling during the early hours of the morning when the work-people were thronging into the city on their way to their daily toil...

Pages:84

Childrens   **ISBN:** *1-59462-373-2*   *MSRP $9.95*

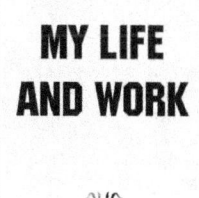

My Life and Work
Henry Ford

QTY

Henry Ford revolutionized the world with his implementation of mass production for the Model T automobile. Gain valuable business insight into his life and work with his own auto-biography... "We have only started on our development of our country we have not as yet, with all our talk of wonderful progress, done more than scratch the surface. The progress has been wonderful enough but..."

Pages:300

Biographies/   **ISBN:** *1-59462-198-5*   *MSRP $21.95*

The Art of Cross-Examination
Francis Wellman

QTY

I presume it is the experience of every author, after his first book is published upon an important subject, to be almost overwhelmed with a wealth of ideas and illustrations which could readily have been included in his book, and which to his own mind, at least, seem to make a second edition inevitable. Such certainly was the case with me; and when the first edition had reached its sixth impression in five months, I rejoiced to learn that it seemed to my publishers that the book had met with a sufficiently favorable reception to justify a second and considerably enlarged edition. ..

Pages:412

Reference   ISBN: *1-59462-647-2*   *MSRP $19.95*

On the Duty of Civil Disobedience
Henry David Thoreau

QTY

Thoreau wrote his famous essay, On the Duty of Civil Disobedience, as a protest against an unjust but popular war and the immoral but popular institution of slave-owning. He did more than write—he declined to pay his taxes, and was hauled off to gaol in consequence. Who can say how much this refusal of his hastened the end of the war and of slavery ?

Law   ISBN: *1-59462-747-9*   **Pages:48**

MSRP $7.45

Dream Psychology Psychoanalysis for Beginners
Sigmund Freud

QTY

Sigmund Freud, born Sigismund Schlomo Freud (May 6, 1856 - September 23, 1939), was a Jewish-Austrian neurologist and psychiatrist who co-founded the psychoanalytic school of psychology. Freud is best known for his theories of the unconscious mind, especially involving the mechanism of repression; his redefinition of sexual desire as mobile and directed towards a wide variety of objects; and his therapeutic techniques, especially his understanding of transference in the therapeutic relationship and the presumed value of dreams as sources of insight into unconscious desires.

Pages:196

Psychology   ISBN: *1-59462-905-6*   *MSRP $15.45*

The Miracle of Right Thought
Orison Swett Marden

QTY

Believe with all of your heart that you will do what you were made to do. When the mind has once formed the habit of holding cheerful, happy, prosperous pictures, it will not be easy to form the opposite habit. It does not matter how improbable or how far away this realization may see, or how dark the prospects may be, if we visualize them as best we can, as vividly as possible, hold tenaciously to them and vigorously struggle to attain them, they will gradually become actualized, realized in the life. But a desire, a longing without endeavor, a yearning abandoned or held indifferently will vanish without realization.

Pages:360

Self Help   ISBN: *1-59462-644-8*   *MSRP $25.45*

www.bookjungle.com *email: sales@bookjungle.com fax: 630-214-0564 mail: Book Jungle PO Box 2226 Champaign, IL 61825*

QTY

The Rosicrucian Cosmo-Conception Mystic Christianity *by Max Heindel* ISBN: *1-59462-188-8* **$38.95**
The Rosicrucian Cosmo-conception is not dogmatic, neither does it appeal to any other authority than the reason of the student. It is: not controversial, but is: sent forth in the, hope that it may help to clear.. New Age/Religion Pages 646

Abandonment To Divine Providence *by Jean-Pierre de Caussade* ISBN: *1-59462-228-0* **$25.95**
"The Rev. Jean Pierre de Caussade was one of the most remarkable spiritual writers of the Society of Jesus in France in the 18th Century. His death took place at Toulouse in 1751. His works have gone through many editions and have been republished... Inspirational/Religion Pages 400

Mental Chemistry *by Charles Haanel* ISBN: *1-59462-192-6* **$23.95**
Mental Chemistry allows the change of material conditions by combining and appropriately utilizing the power of the mind. Much like applied chemistry creates something new and unique out of careful combinations of chemicals the mastery of mental chemistry... New Age Pages 354

The Letters of Robert Browning and Elizabeth Barret Barrett 1845-1846 vol II ISBN: *1-59462-193-4* **$35.95**
by Robert Browning and Elizabeth Barrett Biographies Pages 596

Gleanings In Genesis (volume I) *by Arthur W. Pink* ISBN: *1-59462-130-6* **$27.45**
Appropriately has Genesis been termed "the seed plot of the Bible" for in it we have, in germ form, almost all of the great doctrines which are afterwards fully developed in the books of Scripture which follow... Religion/Inspirational Pages 420

The Master Key *by L. W. de Laurence* ISBN: *1-59462-001-6* **$30.95**
In no branch of human knowledge has there been a more lively increase of the spirit of research during the past few years than in the study of Psychology, Concentration and Mental Discipline. The requests for authentic lessons in Thought Control, Mental Discipline and... New Age/Business Pages 422

The Lesser Key Of Solomon Goetia *by L. W. de Laurence* ISBN: *1-59462-092-X* **$9.95**
This translation of the first book of the "Lernegton" which is now for the first time made accessible to students of Talismanic Magic was done, after careful collation and edition, from numerous Ancient Manuscripts in Hebrew, Latin, and French... New Age/Occult Pages 92

Rubaiyat Of Omar Khayyam *by Edward Fitzgerald* ISBN: *1-59462-332-5* **$13.95**
Edward Fitzgerald, whom the world has already learned, in spite of his own efforts to remain within the shadow of anonymity, to look upon as one of the rarest poets of the century, was born at Bredfield, in Suffolk, on the 31st of March, 1809. He was the third son of John Purcell... Music Pages 172

Ancient Law *by Henry Maine* ISBN: *1-59462-128-4* **$29.95**
The chief object of the following pages is to indicate some of the earliest ideas of mankind, as they are reflected in Ancient Law, and to point out the relation of those ideas to modern thought. Religiom/History Pages 452

Far-Away Stories *by William J. Locke* ISBN: *1-59462-129-2* **$19.45**
"Good wine needs no bush, but a collection of mixed vintages does. And this book is just such a collection. Some of the stories I do not want to remain buried for ever in the museum files of dead magazine-numbers an author's not unpardonable vanity..." Fiction Pages 272

Life of David Crockett *by David Crockett* ISBN: *1-59462-250-7* **$27.45**
"Colonel David Crockett was one of the most remarkable men of the times in which he lived. Born in humble life, but gifted with a strong will, an indomitable courage, and unremitting perseverance... Biographies/New Age Pages 424

Lip-Reading *by Edward Nitchie* ISBN: *1-59462-206-X* **$25.95**
Edward B. Nitchie, founder of the New York School for the Hard of Hearing, now the Nitchie School of Lip-Reading, Inc, wrote "LIP-READING Principles and Practice". The development and perfecting of this meritorious work on lip-reading was an undertaking... How-to Pages 400

A Handbook of Suggestive Therapeutics, Applied Hypnotism, Psychic Science ISBN: *1-59462-214-0* **$24.95**
by Henry Munro Health/New Age/Health/Self-help Pages 376

A Doll's House: and Two Other Plays *by Henrik Ibsen* ISBN: *1-59462-112-8* **$19.95**
Henrik Ibsen created this classic when in revolutionary 1848 Rome. Introducing some striking concepts in playwriting for the realist genre, this play has been studied the world over. Fiction/Classics/Plays 308

The Light of Asia *by sir Edwin Arnold* ISBN: *1-59462-204-3* **$13.95**
In this poetic masterpiece, Edwin Arnold describes the life and teachings of Buddha. The man who was to become known as Buddha to the world was born as Prince Gautama of India but he rejected the worldly riches and abandoned the reigns of power when... Religion/History/Biographies Pages 170

The Complete Works of Guy de Maupassant *by Guy de Maupassant* ISBN: *1-59462-157-8* **$16.95**
"For days and days, nights and nights, I had dreamed of that first kiss which was to consecrate our engagement, and I knew not on what spot I should put my lips..." Fiction/Classics Pages 240

The Art of Cross-Examination *by Francis L. Wellman* ISBN: *1-59462-309-0* **$26.95**
Written by a renowned trial lawyer, Wellman imparts his experience and uses case studies to explain how to use psychology to extract desired information through questioning. How-to/Science/Reference Pages 408

Answered or Unanswered? *by Louisa Vaughan* ISBN: *1-59462-248-5* **$10.95**
Miracles of Faith in China Religion Pages 112

The Edinburgh Lectures on Mental Science (1909) *by Thomas* ISBN: *1-59462-008-3* **$11.95**
This book contains the substance of a course of lectures recently given by the writer in the Queen Street Hall, Edinburgh. Its purpose is to indicate the Natural Principles governing the relation between Mental Action and Material Conditions... New Age/Psychology Pages 148

Ayesha *by H. Rider Haggard* ISBN: *1-59462-301-5* **$24.95**
Verily and indeed it is the unexpected that happens! Probably if there was one person upon the earth from whom the Editor of this, and of a certain previous history, did not expect to hear again... Classics Pages 380

Ayala's Angel *by Anthony Trollope* ISBN: *1-59462-352-X* **$29.95**
The two girls were both pretty, but Lucy who was twenty-one who supposed to be simple and comparatively unattractive, whereas Ayala was credited, as her Bombwhat romantic name might show, with poetic charm and a taste for romance. Ayala when her father died was nineteen... Fiction Pages 484

The American Commonwealth *by James Bryce* ISBN: *1-59462-286-8* **$34.45**
An interpretation of American democratic political theory. It examines political mechanics and society from the perspective of Scotsman James Bryce Politics Pages 572

Stories of the Pilgrims *by Margaret P. Pumphrey* ISBN: *1-59462-116-0* **$17.95**
This book explores pilgrims religious oppression in England as well as their escape to Holland and eventual crossing to America on the Mayflower, and their early days in New England... History Pages 268

QTY

The Fasting Cure *by Sinclair Upton*   **ISBN:** *1-59462-222-1*   **$13.95**

In the Cosmopolitan Magazine for May, 1910, and in the Contemporary Review (London) for April, 1910, I published an article dealing with my experiences in fasting. I have written a great many magazine articles, but never one which attracted so much attention...   New Age/Self Help/Health Pages 164

Hebrew Astrology *by Sepharial*   **ISBN:** *1-59462-308-2*   **$13.45**

In these days of advanced thinking it is a matter of common observation that we have left many of the old landmarks behind and that we are now pressing forward to greater heights and to a wider horizon than that which represented the mind-content of our progenitors...   Astrology Pages 144

Thought Vibration or The Law of Attraction in the Thought World   **ISBN:** *1-59462-127-6*   **$12.95**

by William Walker Atkinson   Psychology/Religion Pages 144

Optimism *by Helen Keller*   **ISBN:** *1-59462-108-X*   **$15.95**

Helen Keller was blind, deaf, and mute since 19 months old, yet famously learned how to overcome these handicaps, communicate with the world, and spread her lectures promoting optimism. An inspiring read for everyone...   Biographies/Inspirational Pages 84

Sara Crewe *by Frances Burnett*   **ISBN:** *1-59462-360-0*   **$9.45**

In the first place, Miss Minchin lived in London. Her home was a large, dull, tall one, in a large, dull square, where all the houses were alike, and all the sparrows were alike, and where all the door-knockers made the same heavy sound...   Childrens/Classic Pages 88

The Autobiography of Benjamin Franklin *by Benjamin Franklin*   **ISBN:** *1-59462-135-7*   **$24.95**

The Autobiography of Benjamin Franklin has probably been more extensively read than any other American historical work, and no other book of its kind has had such ups and downs of fortune. Franklin lived for many years in England, where he was agent...   Biographies/History Pages 332

Name	
Email	
Telephone	
Address	
City, State ZIP	

☐ **Credit Card**   ☐ **Check / Money Order**

Credit Card Number	
Expiration Date	
Signature	

Please Mail to: Book Jungle
PO Box 2226
Champaign, IL 61825
or Fax to: 630-214-0564

ORDERING INFORMATION

web*: www.bookjungle.com*
email*: sales@bookjungle.com*
fax*: 630-214-0564*
mail*: Book Jungle PO Box 2226 Champaign, IL 61825*
or PayPal *to sales@bookjungle.com*

Please contact us for bulk discounts

DIRECT-ORDER TERMS

**20% Discount if You Order
Two or More Books**
Free Domestic Shipping!
Accepted: Master Card, Visa,
Discover, American Express

www.ingramcontent.com/pod-product-compliance
Lightning Source LLC
Chambersburg PA
CBHW081203170626
46813CB00009B/3306